A Junior Novelization

Adapted by Victoria Kosara
Based on the original screenplay
by Elise Allen
Illustrations by Dynamo Limited

taylor

SCHOLASTIC INC.

New York   Toronto   London   Auckland

Sydney   Mexico City   New Delhi   Hong Kong

ISBN 978-0-545-23797-0

BARBIE and associated trademarks and trade dress are owned by,
and used under license from, Mattel, Inc.
© 2010 Mattel, Inc. All Rights Reserved.

Special thanks to Vicki Jaeger, Monica Okazaki, Kathleen Warner, Emily Kelly,
Sarah Quesenberry, Carla Alford, Julia Phelps, Tanya Mann, Rob Hudnut,
Shelley Dvi-Vardhana, Michelle Cogan, Greg Winters,
Taia Morley, and Dynamo Limited

Published by Scholastic Inc.
SCHOLASTIC and associated logos are trademarks and/or registered trademarks of
Scholastic Inc.

12 11 10 9 8 7 6 5 4 3 2 1   10 11 12 13 14/0

Printed in the U.S.A. 40
First printing, October 2010

Chapter 1

A beautiful princess climbed up a ladder leading to a large pile of mattresses. She was very grateful that the queen had given her a place to rest for the night. As she reached the top of the enormous bed, she thanked the queen for being so kind. The queen replied, "But of course, darling! I would provide no less for a princess!" Then the queen turned away and muttered, "If you really are a princess."

Then the queen shouted, "Bring the peas!"

The lights went out and spooky music began to play as four dancing pea zombies came out and started climbing toward the princess's bed!

Luckily for the princess, this scary situation was only a scene in a movie based on the story *The Princess and the Pea* that she was filming. In real life, the princess was being played by Barbie. "Whoa! Time-out!" shouted Barbie. She couldn't take these zombie peas anymore!

"Cut!" said Todd, the director of the movie. "Is there some reason you're interrupting my shot?" he asked Barbie.

"Todd, your vision is so . . . unique. But to me, the story of *The Princess and the Pea* is so great because it's simple. The princess stays true to herself even when it's hard and everyone else doubts her. If the scene gets *too* unique, I think that really cool story will get lost," Barbie answered.

Todd stopped to think for a moment. Finally, he said, "I think I've got the answer. Get off the set! You're fired!"

"I'm *fired*?!" Barbie had never been fired before. As she walked off the set, the actors continued to film without her. When Barbie reached her dressing room, her two best friends, Grace and Teresa, were there to comfort her.

"I can't believe I was fired," said Barbie sadly. "And to make things worse, I saw Todd's assistant spilling the news to the gossip sites as I left the set."

The three friends opened a laptop to check the comments on the Internet. They were not good.

"Those people are happy I got fired!"

Barbie told Grace and Teresa. "If people don't want to see me act . . . well, maybe I shouldn't be acting." Barbie frowned.

Grace said, "Let people talk. It doesn't matter what they say."

Just then, Barbie's phone rang. No name popped up on the caller ID screen, but when she answered, she heard her boyfriend Ken's voice.

"We need to talk," Ken said.

"Ken! I'm *so* glad you called. I—" Barbie tried to tell him what had happened, but Ken just kept talking. It was as if he wasn't even listening to her.

"Things aren't right with us and you know it. They haven't been for a while. I'm breaking up with you . . . right now. It's over. If you're smart, you'll forget I exist," Ken finished.

"Ken, wait! I don't underst—" But the phone clicked off. Barbie was shocked.

"What happened?" asked Grace.

"Ken just broke up with me," said Barbie.

"I don't believe it! That's not like Ken at all," Teresa added.

Barbie tried to call Ken back so that she could talk to him, but the call went right to Ken's voice mail. Grace grabbed Barbie's cell phone away from her. "Teresa and I are getting you someplace far away from this set, where you can feel good about yourself," she said.

Barbie thought for a moment and then had a great idea!

"My aunt Millicent is a designer in Paris with her own fashion house. I loved visiting when I was little. I can spend the last weeks of summer vacation with her. This is just

what I need right now—to be surrounded by tons of people, energy, clothes . . . and Aunt Millicent," Barbie said.

Teresa and Grace helped Barbie book her flight, and Barbie and her poodle, Sequin, boarded the next plane for Paris.

One long flight later, Barbie and Sequin were walking down the streets of Paris toward Aunt Millicent's. On their way up the sidewalk, Barbie and Sequin passed a trendy fashion house.

"*Bonjour, mademoiselle.* Good morning, miss," said the woman, whose name was Jacqueline. She told Barbie that she owned the fashion house that they were standing in front of.

"Thank you!" Barbie answered. "You're a designer? So you must know Millicent's?" Jacqueline and her assistant, Delphine, laughed.

"Jacqueline *ruined* Millicent's!" Delphine told Barbie with an evil grin.

"Delphine, you flatter me," said Jacqueline. "But it's true. See for yourself." The two designers spun around and walked back into their fashion house.

Barbie didn't want to believe Jacqueline. But when Barbie opened the door to Aunt Millicent's fashion house, the room was dark and filled with boxes.

Chapter 2

"I don't get it. I can't get through to Barbie at all!" Ken said to his friend Raquelle. They were sitting at everyone's favorite diner. Ken was helping Raquelle practice her lines for an audition. Raquelle was hoping to become a teen movie star—just like Barbie. But unlike Barbie, Raquelle wasn't a very nice person. And it was no secret she had a huge crush on Ken.

"I'm sure everything's fine," Raquelle said with a smirk. "You know, you are the best for helping me run lines again." Raquelle pulled out a tape recorder.

"It's cool," Ken said. "But do you have to record it this time?"

"This helps me practice when you're not with me," answered Raquelle.

Then Grace and Teresa walked into the diner and caught Ken with Raquelle. They assumed the two were out on a date.

"Are you kidding me?!" Grace scolded Ken.

"Grace! Teresa!" Ken looked happy to see them. "Where's Barbie? I can't reach her at all. Is she okay?"

Teresa and Grace could not believe what they were hearing. "Barbie is fine. She just doesn't want anything to do with the guy who dumped her," Grace snapped.

"Dumped her?!" Ken said, surprised.

Raquelle started to try to sneak away.

"Barbie told us what you said on the phone: 'It's over. If you're smart, you'll forget I exist,'" said Grace.

Ken frowned and looked at Raquelle. He was angry. "Raquelle, that line! It's part of what I read for you yesterday."

"Oh, is it?" said Raquelle.

Ken thought for a moment. "And you recorded it. . . . Don't tell me you played it back to Barbie, and now she thinks that I broke up with her?"

"It was just a joke," Raquelle said.

Ken ignored Raquelle and quickly asked Teresa and Grace where Barbie was. When they explained that she was in Paris, Ken thought for a moment. Then he had a great idea.

"I'll book the next flight to Paris," he said. "I've got to get to Barbie right away!"

Chapter 3

Meanwhile, Barbie and Sequin walked deeper into Aunt Millicent's fashion house. "Hello?" she called into the dark room. Just then, she saw a hot-pink blur speed by. Aunt Millicent was on roller skates! "Aunt Millicent!" yelled Barbie.

Aunt Millicent skated over to Barbie and hugged her. Out of the corner of her eye, Barbie saw a girl walking down the steps.

"Alice, this is my niece, Barbie," Aunt Millicent said.

"Nice to meet you, Barbie," said Alice.

Barbie also noticed Sequin barking playfully at Aunt Millicent's cat, Jilliana, and her Jack Russell terrier, Jacques. Then Barbie turned to her aunt and asked her why everything was packed in boxes. Millicent looked sad as she said, "I didn't want to tell you on the phone, but I'm closing up the shop and moving to the country!"

Barbie was confused. Her aunt had made some of the best clothes in Paris! How could she close her fashion house? "So, Jacqueline was right. . . ." she whispered.

Alice frowned. "Jacqueline?! She cheats! She copies the real designers, like Millicent, and then spends all her time and money getting the newspapers and TV stations to notice her. They love her, and they won't pay attention to anyone else. It's just not fair," she explained.

Aunt Millicent shook her head. "Oh, they pay attention to me. It's just the things they have to say. They're horrible. They call me 'washed up' and say my designs are 'old.'"

"No!" Barbie told her. "I've seen your latest designs. They are fabulous!"

Aunt Millicent looked sad. "Well, not according to my audience. So, I ask you, if your audience does not like what you make, does it make sense to keep designing?"

Barbie thought for a moment. That's exactly what had happened to her. She remembered how hurt she had been by what people had said about her online. Barbie said, "No. No, it doesn't."

"See, Alice?" Aunt Millicent said. "I told you Barbie would understand. We think alike," she said to Barbie. Barbie smiled, but Alice just shook her head.

"Well, I have a lot of packing to do," said Aunt Millicent. "The new owners will be here in two days."

Barbie offered to help pack up. It was the least she could do for her favorite aunt. Alice and Barbie headed upstairs to the studio.

"Can you believe Aunt Millicent sold her fashion house to a guy who is going to make hot dogs in here?" Alice said.

"What?" Barbie was shocked. "But it's so magical here."

Suddenly, Alice stopped packing, too. "Magical? Did you say it was magical?"

Barbie blushed. "I know it sounds silly, but when I was little, I always felt like all your dreams could come true here."

Alice smiled. "It's not silly! That's exactly what I think." She ran over to another staircase. "I have to show you something," Alice said with excitement.

Barbie followed Alice up the steps into a beautiful old room that looked even more magical than the studio. It had a worktable and a clothing rack with one beautiful dress hanging on it.

"Wow!" said Barbie.

"I know," Alice said. "I wasn't going to say anything because I thought you'd think I was crazy. But then when you said that you think this place is magical, well . . ."

Barbie walked over to the dress. "I knew that the Paris press was crazy. This dress is totally awesome! Just like all of Aunt Millicent's designs."

"You really think so?" Alice asked Barbie.

"Of course! Don't you?"

Alice shrugged. "It's hard to say. This

actually isn't one of Millicent's dresses. It was inspired by her, but I designed it myself," she said softly.

Barbie smiled. "Really? I didn't know you're a designer, too!"

"Well, I'm not really. It's just a little something I tried," Alice said.

"Wow. In this musty old attic, all by yourself? It's like the beginning of a fairytale!" said Barbie.

"I love working up here because of the history . . . and the magic. Come look!" Alice walked to the other side of the attic. She pushed away a tarp. Behind it was an old wardrobe.

"Oh, wow," Barbie teased. "You made a wardrobe appear."

Alice giggled. "No! That's not it." Alice turned and grabbed an old, dusty book

from behind her. "Look at this picture. It's the wardrobe that's right here. This book says that this building was the home of the very first fashion house in Paris! It's been a fashion house for over two hundred years. And this book even has stories about the magic that's here. *Real* magic!"

"Well, it does look like the same wardrobe," said Barbie.

"It is! And look. The book says that there

are magical creatures who appeared from inside an old wardrobe to help designers over the years. It's *this* wardrobe. It's magical!" Alice carefully opened one door of the wardrobe. It was dark and empty, and it kind of smelled funny.

"I read that you can call the magical creatures in two steps. First you put a worthy design in the wardrobe. It has to be something that the designer made with her heart." Alice picked up her dress and held it out in front of her. "I don't know if it's worthy, but it's the only thing we have."

"What's the second step?" asked Barbie, unsure if the wardrobe was magical.

"We have to recite a chant," Alice explained. "The book says that the writing is on the wall, but I can't find it anywhere!"

Barbie looked around for a clue. She

noticed a strange-looking handle. She tugged on it, and part of the wall slid away!

"You found it!" Alice said, clapping her hands.

"Alice, put in your dress. Quick!" Alice carefully put her dress into the wardrobe and closed the door.

Together, the girls recited the French chant written on the wall, which translated to "With inspiration, love, and care, great fashions earn the glow of flair. Some shimmer, glimmer, and some shine bring life and sparkles every time."

Barbie and Alice spun around and stared at the wardrobe. It looked exactly the same. Alice frowned sadly. Barbie sighed.

"I was so sure," said Alice. "But maybe my dress isn't worthy enough. I told you, I'm not really a designer." The girls headed for the stairs, but Barbie saw a sparkle as she was turning to leave.

"Alice, wait! Look!" Barbie said, pointing to the wardrobe. There were beautiful lights dancing behind the closed doors of the wardrobe. The lights grew brighter and brighter until the doors of the wardrobe suddenly swung open. Three magical creatures appeared dressed in fashionable outfits. They were tiny like fairies, but they didn't have any wings.

"Flairies, fall in!" shouted Shyne, the middle creature. The beautiful Flairies followed a path of sparkle dust to bring themselves closer to the girls.

"The magical creatures," Alice gasped.

"Creatures? Where?!" the Flairy named Glimmer asked.

"I hope you don't mean us," said Shyne.

"We are not creatures. We're Flairies! I'm Shyne, and this is Shimmer and Glimmer," she said, pointing to her friends.

"Oh," Barbie said. "You're fairies."

"No, girl! Fairies have wings," Shyne explained.

"We're *Flairies*. We have . . . flair!" Glimmer said as she struck a pose.

"A flair we share!" said Shimmer. "And now . . . look!" The Flairies moved out of the way so that Barbie and Alice could see the wardrobe. Alice's dress was glowing with sparkle!

"My dress!" Alice exclaimed.

"Oh, so *you're* the designer," said Shyne. "A pleasure working with you."

"Me?" Alice asked. "I just made a plain dress. You made it fabulous!"

Shimmer giggled. "Oh, don't be silly.

Our magic only works on designs that inspire us."

"Right," said Glimmer. "It only works *well* that way. If we use it on bad designs, well, it's usually not good."

"Exactly!" Shyne said. "We come when we're called, and if we like what we see, we add shimmer, glimmer, and shine."

"So, when you're not called, you live in the wardrobe?"

"We call it the glitterizer, but no."

Shimmer laughed. "We travel! We go where we're summoned and help designers all over the world!"

Shyne explained, "We came to life in this fashion house. It's the source of our powers, but it's not where we live."

"Wait! If the fashion house is the source of your powers, would it be really, really bad if someone else bought it, cleaned it out, and made it a hot dog restaurant?" Barbie looked concerned.

The Flairies laughed. "A hot dog place! That is so funny. I thought you were serious for a minute." Shimmer couldn't stop laughing. But when she saw that Glimmer and Shyne were not smiling, Shimmer asked, "It *is* a joke, right?"

Alice shook her head. "No. I wish it were a joke, too."

Glimmer looked like she was going to cry. "But, Shyne, if the fashion house isn't a fashion house anymore, won't we lose our powers?"

"Not on my watch!" Shyne shouted. She put her hands on her hips. "Well, who is in charge here? We have to find a way to save this place."

Alice answered, "Millicent, and she's down in her office, but—" Before she could finish, the Flairies were on their way downstairs.

Alice grabbed her glamorous dress, and the two girls raced down the stairs. Alice and Barbie burst into Aunt Millicent's office, just before the Flairies could get there.

"Aunt Millicent!" Barbie yelled as she and Alice entered the room.

Aunt Millicent immediately noticed

Alice's sparkling dress. "Now that is a fabulous dress! Where did you find that?" she asked, pointing to the dress. It was still glowing.

"Alice designed it!" Barbie said.

"It's so beautiful. And the sparkle!" Aunt Millicent was glowing, too.

But Alice hadn't forgotten about the Flairies. "Millicent, remember how I told you there were magical creatures in this house, and you thought I was crazy?" Alice was speaking as fast as she could. "Well, maybe I wasn't so crazy."

Just then, Shyne yelled into the room, "We must talk to Millicent!" Glimmer and Shimmer followed behind her. The three Flairies stopped right in front of Aunt Millicent. "We have a bone to pick with you."

"What in the world?" Aunt Millicent

could not believe what she was seeing. Barbie explained they were Flairies, and how they were the ones who added sparkle to Alice's dress. "That's their power, and they've done it for over two hundred years!" Barbie finished.

"Yes," said Shyne. "But if this place becomes a hot dog stand, then that magic goes *kaplooie*! Forever."

The room went silent. "Right now, there's nothing I can do," Aunt Millicent said. "I've already sold the building. I'd have to design and sell a whole new fashion line to make enough money to buy it back."

That gave Barbie a great idea!

"Could you make a new fashion line?" Barbie looked up at Aunt Millicent.

"By the end of the day on Friday?!" Aunt Millicent shook her head. "Not a chance.

And even if I could, people don't like my work anymore, remember?"

Aunt Millicent turned to the Flairies. "I'm sorry. Truly sorry. But I'm afraid I can't help you," she said as she left the room.

"So that's it," Glimmer said.

Shimmer added, "Come Saturday morning . . . no more powers."

Suddenly, the front door flew open. "That *dress*!" A beautiful woman dressed in very fashionable clothes walked in. Shimmer, Glimmer, and Shyne quickly hid out of sight. "I've never seen anything like it!" The woman circled the dress form, looking at the beautiful dress.

"Of course not! It's a supremely exclusive original from Mademoiselle Alice, Millicent's top new designer," Barbie explained. Alice's jaw dropped. "You're the

first to see it . . . so far," Barbie added.

"I must have it! How much?" she said as she spun around to face Barbie.

"Tough call," said Barbie. "It's a very choice design." Barbie showed the woman the price on a piece of paper. Alice was shocked that the woman would pay that much for her design.

"It's a steal! I'll take it," the woman said. "And don't bother with a bag. I'm going to wear it home. I want the whole world to see me in this dress!" She beamed at Alice. The woman paid and glided out the door. The dress glittered as she walked.

When the door was closed, the Flairies flew out from hiding. Everyone was so excited!

"Can you imagine if you had a whole line of dresses like that?" Barbie asked. "You could—" She gasped. "Wait! Aunt Millicent said that she can't make and sell a fashion line by Friday . . . but you can, Alice!"

Shyne grinned. "Now *that* is a plan!"

"Ooh! And you can have a big fashion show on Friday night to show off the outfits," Shimmer suggested.

Glimmer added, "*And* raise enough money to save Millicent's fashion house and our powers!"

Chapter 4

Alice and Barbie got right to work. When Alice finished her designs, the girls walked over to the wardrobe where the outfits were hanging. Barbie closed the doors of the wardrobe carefully and together they chanted, "With inspiration, love, and care, great fashions earn the glow of flair. Some shimmer, glimmer, and some shine bring life and sparkles every time."

The Flairies were inspired by Alice's designs.

31

"Shine!" said Shyne.

"Shimmer!" said Shimmer.

"Glimmer!" said Glimmer as she tried to shoot out Flairy dust. It transformed into a small explosion of color before it hit the dresses. "I'm still kind of working on my part," she said.

Barbie and Alice watched as a burst of colors exploded behind the doors of the wardrobe. Once the flash of magic ended, Alice walked over to the wardrobe. She slowly opened each door and stood back.

Each dress glittered and glowed. They were the most beautiful dresses Barbie had ever seen. Barbie and Alice jumped up and down from excitement. Barbie hugged Alice.

"You did it!" She beamed at Alice.

"*We* did it," Alice said to Barbie and the Flairies.

Just then, Aunt Millicent walked into the studio. When she saw the dresses her jaw dropped. "These dresses!" She walked closer and touched one of the glittering designs. "Alice, did you make these?" She turned to Alice.

Alice looked down at her feet nervously. "Well, the Flairies really brought them to life," she told Aunt Millicent.

Barbie ran over to stand next to Alice. "Yes, but they're Alice's original designs!" She smiled.

"Do you like them?" Alice looked up at Aunt Millicent.

"Like them?" Aunt Millicent said. "I *love* them! With these dresses, you could work at any fashion house in Paris."

Alice's eyes lit up and she smiled. Alice was glowing like her dresses.

"I know we should be packing, but we're just not ready to give up on Millicent's fashion house and the Flairies yet," Barbie said to Aunt Millicent. "You did say a great fashion line could make enough money to save the place, right?"

But Aunt Millicent was not listening. She had wandered over to the inspiration photos that Alice pinned up when they had started working earlier that day.

"These are from my very first fashion line," said Aunt Millicent.

"These inspire me," said Alice. She moved closer to Aunt Millicent. "Your work always has." They looked at each other. It was quiet for a moment.

"Inspires her like crazy!" Barbie chimed in. "You wouldn't believe how many ideas she has. Totally enough for a huge fashion show here on Friday night . . . if you'll let us do it."

Aunt Millicent knew that the girls had worked hard, and she smiled. But then the smile disappeared. "You know what a fashion show really is?" Aunt Millicent asked the girls. "It's an invitation to be eaten alive. What if people don't show up? What if they judge you and write horrible things for everyone to read?"

Everyone was quiet. Suddenly, Alice smiled again. "I guess I'll have to be happy that I did what I love, and I did the best I could." She turned to Barbie, who smiled back. "Actually," Alice stammered shyly to Aunt Millicent, "I was hoping maybe you'd want to work together on this."

Aunt Millicent gave Alice a big hug. "Alice, I would be honored to work with you. But the last thing you need is my reputation bringing you down. You girls can do your own fashion show here, but please, don't be too disappointed if it doesn't go the way you hope," she said.

Alice and Barbie nodded.

"So," said Aunt Millicent with a smile, "how about you two take a break and join me upstairs for dinner?"

"Yes, I'm starved!" Barbie answered.

Chapter 5

The next day, Jacqueline stared out her window at the new outfits in Millicent's front window. She was surprised.

"It makes no sense. Millicent's fashion house is closing. She has no designers. But those outfits in the window . . . they are magnificent! Like nothing I've ever seen before. *C'est impossible!* How can it be?"

"That's funny," said Delphine. "You think the outfits are impossible. But," she said, pointing, "I think what's impossible are the teeny-tiny models floating through the air on sparkles."

"What?!" Jacqueline gasped. She grabbed the binoculars. "Where?" Jacqueline spotted the Flairies by a superhip, funky dress that Alice had just finished. Shimmer and Shyne shot Flairy dust onto the latest design, and it glittered. Jacqueline was speechless. "Incredible!" she whispered.

"What are they?" Delphine asked.

"I don't know," said Jacqueline. "But they are responsible for the new style at Millicent's . . . which means I have to make them mine."

"But how?" asked Delphine.

"We just have to wait for the right moment," Jacqueline said.

Jacqueline and Delphine waited all day for the perfect time to steal the Flairies.

Finally Barbie and Alice left the studio for a break at the café next door. Once the girls were gone, Jacqueline and Delphine snuck into Millicent's.

Very quietly, the two snuck up the stairs. They stopped when they spotted the Flairies. They were playing jump rope and singing, "Sparkle shower, that's our power. We glow clothes that always —" The Flairies could not finish their rhyme, as Jacqueline caught them in a pillowcase in one scoop.

"Alert! Alert!" yelled Shyne.

"Ambush!" Shimmer shouted.

"What's going on?" Glimmer asked. They were trapped!

Jacqueline held the top of the pillowcase tightly closed. An evil grin spread across her face. "Come on, Delphine!" she whispered. "We've got them!"

The two snuck out of Millicent's fashion house. Once they were safely inside Jacqueline's, Delphine emptied the Flairies into a birdcage. Jacqueline slammed the door shut and locked it before they could get out.

"Get back, Flairy-nappers!" Shyne yelled. "You have no idea who you're dealing with." Shyne did some karate kicks

and jumps and landed with her arms up in
a pose.

Jacqueline looked into the cage. "I'll let
you out at some point," she said. "But not
until you help me."

Shyne said, "Aha! A ransom situation.
What's your price?"

Jacqueline laughed. "Simple," she said

to the Flairies. "You glitterize *my* designs, like you did to the ones at Millicent's, and I'll let you go." Then she turned to Delphine. "Delphine, bring over my latest designs!"

"Um," Delphine whispered, "we don't really have anything new. Without Millicent designing, we didn't have anything to copy, so . . ."

"Well, we have to have *something*!" Jacqueline yelled. "Just grab whatever you can find, and they'll make it look good."

Delphine ran back with an armful of dull fabrics and dropped them in front of the Flairies' cage. The clothes were not pretty. Glimmer, Shimmer, and Shyne stared at the pile of ugly designs. How could they use their magic on something that did not inspire them at all?

"I got nothing," Shyne said to the other Flairies. "You?"

Shimmer and Glimmer shook their heads. Still, they wanted to get out of the cage, so Glimmer spoke to Jacqueline. "Hey, maybe you should go to the fashion show at Millicent's tomorrow night. Alice's designs are incredible! You could learn a lot."

Jacqueline looked mad. *"Excusez-moi!"* she shouted. "I won't go to Millicent's fashion show because I'll be here having my *own* fashion show. Now make with the magic so I can get the word out."

Shyne, Shimmer, and Glimmer stared back at Jacqueline, then looked down at her boring designs again. "Here's the deal," Shyne finally said. "We're not inspired by these dresses. If we 'make with the magic,' we don't know what will happen . . . but it probably won't be good."

Jacqueline crossed her arms. "You're just stalling!" she yelled into the cage.

"She's not," Glimmer said softly. "It's true."

"Yeah, you really don't want us to do it," Shimmer added.

Jacqueline was really angry now. She turned around to Delphine, who held a bottle of perfume.

"Spritz them!" Jacqueline shouted.

Delphine walked toward the cage and showered the Flairies in smelly perfume.

"Oh no!" Shimmer coughed. "Cheap perfume!"

"Okay!" Shyne yelled. "We'll do it!"

"Excellent!" Jacqueline clapped.

"Just remember," Shyne said, "we

warned you." Shyne's Flairy dust shot down
to the pile of Jacqueline's designs. "Shine!"
she said. The dresses shined.

"Shimmer!" shouted Shimmer. Her
Flairy dust landed on the pile, and the
dresses shimmered brightly. Glimmer
tried to add her magic to the designs, but
her magic faded before it reached the pile.
Still, the dresses were glowing, just like the
ones that were in Aunt Millicent's window.

Jacqueline beamed. "I knew you were stalling," said Jacqueline. "My dresses are beautiful!"

With the latest glowing style, Jacqueline would be able to stay in business, and Millicent would be out of the fashion world for good. She moved the Flairies' cage up to a high shelf.

"These dresses are perfect, just like all my dresses will be from now on. Thanks to you, my pets," Jacqueline said to the Flairies.

"But—" Glimmer shook the door of the cage. "You said you'd let us out of here if we glitterized your dresses, and we did!"

Jacqueline just laughed. "Come, Delphine. We must prepare." The two women raced out of the room to get ready for their fashion show.

Chapter 6

I
DED
DO
thev on

io ͡ r

rrFiS

ToIY

(OR

Barbie and Alice returned from the café.

"Shyne! Shimmer! Glimmer!" Barbie shouted. "We're back."

When the Flairies didn't answer, Barbie and Alice began to look for them. "Shyne? Glimmer? Shimmer?" they called. Still there was no answer.

"Look out below!" yelled Aunt Millicent.

Barbie looked up to see her aunt hanging from the ceiling! Aunt Millicent had on

ers and was climbing along
t Millicent!" said Barbie,

enly, Aunt Millicent let go. She
to land gracefully, but she plopped
o a pile of fabric. "I'm fine! I was
practicing a French sport called parkour."

"What?" Barbie asked.

"I got an idea for these sneakers, and I
had to try it out. They're cute, right?" Aunt
Millicent smiled.

Barbie looked at her aunt's shoes. They
were some of the best-looking sneakers
she had ever seen. "You are the coolest aunt
in the world!" Barbie hugged her.

Aunt Millicent bowed and giggled.
"Thank you!"

"Aunt Millicent," Barbie said, "have you
seen the Flairies? They weren't up in the

apartment with you, were they?"

"No," answered Aunt Millicent.

Just then, Alice came down from th
attic. She looked worried. "They aren't up
in the attic either. They're gone!"

Barbie shook her head. "We're trying to
save their power. Why would they leave?"

Alice said, "What if they had to? Maybe
they were called somewhere else. But still,
what are we going to do? The fashion show is
tomorrow, and we have more new designs.
We can't do it without the Flairies' magic."

"Well . . ." Aunt Millicent looked at
Alice. "Maybe I can help instead."

"Really?!" Barbie smiled. "But last night
you said—"

Aunt Millicent waved her arm. "Oh, I
know what I said, and I meant it," Aunt
Millicent told the girls. "People haven't

...ions at all lately, but I *love* ... Aunt Millicent pointed to her ...ers. "I clearly can't stop." She ... "Plus, I'm newly inspired ... by ...lice."

By me?" Alice asked with excitement.

Aunt Millicent nodded. "Yes, Alice. You're brave enough to follow your passion no matter what people might say. That's true style ... and I've always fancied myself a woman of style!" she said.

"Hello," Barbie chimed in. "You're the most stylish woman on the planet, Aunt Millicent!"

"*Oui!*" Alice agreed. "You're *my* inspiration. To design with you is a dream come true!"

Aunt Millicent clapped and smiled. "Wonderful! So it's settled, then. What time is this fashion show tomorrow?"

"Eight o'clock," said Barbie.

"Perfect!" Aunt Millicent answered. "That's just enough time to never in a million years make a whole new fashion line. Now, who's up for the challenge?"

"I am!" Barbie shouted.

"*Oui!* Me too!" Alice beamed.

Aunt Millicent laughed. "Then let's get to work!"

The team worked late into the night, cutting, pinning, sewing, and laughing while they helped Alice put together her beautiful new designs. Finally, they were finished. Maybe they could have a great fashion show after all.

Chapter 7

While the designers slept, the Flairies sat in their cage. Finally, Shyne had an idea.

"Millicent's is right across the street!" Shyne reminded them. "We need to make sparks! If anyone is awake, they'll see our fireworks and rescue us!"

Shimmer jumped up. "That's a great idea!"

All three took a deep breath and walked to the edge of the cage. "Ready?" Shyne asked. "Shine!" she shouted.

"Shimmer!"

"Glimmer!" Glimmer yelled as loudly as she could. Her dust did nothing, but Shyne's and Shimmer's Flairy dust exploded into superbright, colorful fireworks right in front of the window.

Suddenly, the Flairies spotted a head in Millicent's window. It was Sequin!

"It's perfect," Shyne said. "And just the right dog is awake to see it."

Sequin blinked her eyes and stared

at the fireworks. She realized who had made the bright lights. *The Flairies!* she thought. Sequin shook Jilliana and Jacques awake and showed them the window. They realized that the Flairies were trapped in Jacqueline's. The pets knew exactly what they needed to do.

The three animals quietly stood in front of Jacqueline's. Jilliana hopped on top of

Sequin's back and tried to open the front door. It was locked. Jilliana thought of another plan. She climbed up to a window. Jilliana slipped inside, while Sequin and Jacques waited by the front door.

"What is that?" asked Glimmer. She heard a scratching sound.

"Could it be?" Shimmer asked. Just then, Jilliana came into the room.

"Jilliana!" Shimmer shouted happily.

"Here, kitty, kitty!" Shyne called to Jilliana.

Jilliana walked over to the cage quickly. The cage was locked, too. Jilliana tried each one of her claws in the keyhole. Finally, the lock popped open!

"Good, good kitty!" Shimmer said as the Flairies hugged Jilliana.

"Beauty, brains, and brawn," said Shyne. "Now *that's* stylish!"

Then they quietly escaped to Millicent's.

Once they were safe inside Millicent's fashion house, they saw Barbie, Alice, and Millicent sleeping. Glimmer noticed that there were some new designs in the room. "No wonder they are all so tired!" she said. Surrounding them was a full fashion line of amazing dresses. "These are all so perfect, they don't even need any help!"

"Well, maybe just a little glitterizing. But that's it!" Shimmer said with a grin.

Shyne shook her head. "The clothes don't need us, but this room could use some serious shimmer, glimmer, and shine." The three Flairies could make this the coolest fashion studio ever!

Chapter 8

On the day of the fashion show, Ken's plane finally landed in Paris. It had been a rough trip. He'd had to ride in a truck with pigs and sit between two guys in giant pea costumes for his entire flight. But it was all worth it as long as he got to see Barbie. As he left the airport, Ken called for a taxi. "Please take me to Millicent's fashion house," Ken told the driver.

"*Oui!*" the driver answered, and they sped away.

Meanwhile, the designers at Aunt Millicent's were just waking up. Barbie looked around the studio and gasped. "No way! No way!" she shouted.

The studio had been turned into the hippest and most fabulous studio they had ever seen. It was like something from a dream. There was a long catwalk and a stage with a beautiful pink curtain. Even the wardrobe itself had been glitterized.

"This is beyond the coolest thing ever!" Barbie shouted.

"But I don't understand . . . how?" Aunt Millicent wondered.

Suddenly, the Flairies floated into the room. "Shyne, Shimmer, and Glimmer, at your service, ma'am," said Shyne.

Barbie grinned. "You came back!"

"Well," said Shyne, "we really didn't leave."

Shimmer yelled, "We were Flairy-napped!"

Alice ran to the wardrobe and threw open the doors. Sure enough, all the new designs glowed with the Flairies' magic. "Hooray! We can have our fashion show tonight!" Alice said, hopping up and down.

"We barely touched those clothes. Your designs were already perfect as they were. Now, the room, well, that needed some work," said Shyne.

"We are *so* saving this place"—Barbie smiled at the Flairies—"and your powers!" Everyone beamed. Aunt Millicent looked at the clock and said, "Well, let's get ready!"

While everyone continued working their magic at Aunt Millicent's, Jacqueline walked into her fashion house.

"Bonjour, Flairies! I've called in every favor, and everyone who's anyone is on their way to my fashion show right now. Are you excited?"

"They're gone," Delphine told Jacqueline, pointing to the empty cage.

Jacqueline didn't blink. "Hmm. That's too bad, but no matter. Once I show these dresses, I will forever be known as the top designer in all of Paris."

Later, Jacqueline's fashion house was packed with Paris's top designers, newspaper journalists, and television reporters.

Jacqueline walked onto the stage. The whole room clapped. "Thank you, ladies and gentlemen! As you all know, I have long been the toast of Paris. But this collection is the icing on the cake of my career. I call it 'Just Rewards.'" The crowd clapped again, and the lights went black. Jacqueline went backstage.

The models came out in Jacqueline's designs, but something was horribly wrong! Delphine gasped. "Um, Jacqueline?" she said.

"Not now, Delphine. I am breathing in the sweet smell of my success!" Jacqueline exclaimed.

"But, Jacqueline . . ." Delphine said.

Jacqueline sniffed the air. "Why does the sweet smell of my success smell like a gym sock?"

"Jacqueline!" Delphine shouted.

The two watched the models onstage.

Each dress changed into garbage as the models strutted down the runway. Greasy banana peels, dry chicken bones, and used trash bags lined the stage.

"No!" Jacqueline gasped.

"It's the Flairies' magic," Delphine said. "They said it wasn't stable."

"No!" Jacqueline said again. "This can't be happening!"

The audience began to notice the trash on the stage.

"Ugh!" said one magazine writer. "That *smell*! Gross!"

A supermodel made a face. "I've heard of trashy clothes, but this is crazy!"

Suddenly, the audience noticed a glimmering pink light coming from Millicent's window across the street.

"I say we go check out Millicent's. Who's

with me?" asked a newspaper writer.

Then the whole crowd got up and walked to the door. Jacqueline ran back onstage.

"No! Wait! I was tricked! Come back. This was supposed to be my masterpiece, my Just Rewards!" she shouted. But the crowd walked right out the door and crossed the street to Millicent's fashion house.

Chapter 9

Back at Millicent's, everything was ready. It was nearly time for the show to begin, but there was only one person in the audience. It was the hot dog restaurant owner, and he wore a giant hot dog costume. But even if no one showed up, Alice and Barbie were proud that they had made all these beautiful designs. And Aunt Millicent had remembered what she loved to do — design.

Aunt Millicent walked up to the man in

the giant hot dog costume. "*Monsieur!* So glad you came."

"Do you really think you can make enough money tonight to stop me from tearing this place down?" he asked.

Aunt Millicent shrugged. "You gave me your price. I'll do the best I can."

Suddenly, the front door swung open. A huge crowd flooded the room, and soon every seat in the fashion house was taken.

"Yes!" Barbie shouted. "It's packed! The whole room is packed!"

Barbie turned back to Aunt Millicent and Alice. "Are you nervous?" she asked.

"Yes," Alice answered.

"Me too," said Aunt Millicent.

"You're nervous?!" Alice asked. "But you've been doing this forever!"

Barbie answered for her. "Yeah, but

when people say horrible things about you, it can still make you doubt yourself. That's kind of why I came out here."

"Is it?" Aunt Millicent asked.

Barbie nodded. "But it was crazy. Acting is my dream. I can't give up on it just because some people didn't like what I was doing. It's the same for both of you. You're *amazing* designers. And no matter what happens down there tonight, your line is a major success," Barbie told Aunt Millicent and Alice. The three of them hugged.

Then the DJ changed the music. That meant the show was about to start!

"Let's rock this party!" Barbie shouted, and ran down the stairs. The lights in the room faded, and the spotlight lit up the stage. Barbie walked right into the middle of the stage to welcome everyone.

"Tonight, Millicent's fashion house presents a very special line that celebrates staying true to your passion, even when it's hard and everyone else doubts you. It reminds me of a story I once knew," Barbie said. She was thinking of *The Princess and the Pea*. "We call this 'A Fashion Fairytale'!"

Barbie walked backstage, and the lights and music came on. The models strolled down the runway in the glittering designs.

When it was Barbie's turn to walk down the runway, she noticed Jacqueline and Delphine watching from the back.

Soon the show was almost over. Barbie put on her final outfit and walked onstage. The crowd went wild. The Flairies watched from above and smiled.

"How about we finish this off with a bang?" asked Glimmer.

Shyne and Shimmer looked surprised. Glimmer wasn't usually into big bangs.

Shyne was beaming. "I like your attitude!"

The Flairies floated down toward the catwalk and landed right next to Barbie.

"Shine!" Shyne shouted as she shot Flairy dust on the dress.

"Shimmer!" Shimmer said.

"Glimmer!" Glimmer said, concentrating

very hard on the dress.

But instead of the dress just being enhanced, it was entirely transformed! The entire audience gasped, but no one was as shocked as Glimmer.

Shimmer turned to her and said, "Glimmer! You didn't just enhance that dress, you transformed it!"

"I know! I just imagined what I wanted it to look like . . . and that's what it became!" Glimmer said excitedly. She realized then that she had finally found her true talent.

Barbie twirled on the runway one last time. The crowd was clapping and smiling. The music ended, and Barbie walked back to the middle of the stage. Just before she turned to head back down the runway, Barbie looked up at the door. She rubbed her eyes because she could not believe who was standing there. It was Ken!

"Barbie!" he shouted.

Ken made his way through the parting crowd. He looked really tired. His hair was a mess, his clothes were torn, and he smelled kind of gross. "Barbie!" he shouted again. Ken ran over to her and swept her into a big hug.

"Barbie, I would never break up with

you," Ken said. "I didn't! I promise you it was all a misunderstanding. The minute I found out, I knew I had to see you and talk to you, but you had already left and . . ." Ken stopped talking. For the first time, he realized where he was. He noticed the beautiful stage, the well-dressed crowd, and Barbie's glowing gown. "Um, did I come at a bad time?" he asked.

Barbie laughed. "No, you came at the perfect time. And all the way to Paris," Barbie said. "It's the most romantic thing I could ever imagine!"

Ken grinned. "That's exactly what I wanted. A grand romantic gesture to prove how much I love you. And I really do," he told her.

"I love you, too," Barbie answered.

Ken and Barbie kissed. When the Flairies

saw, they sprinkled Flairy dust down on Ken. As soon as the magical dust hit him, Ken was cleaned up and glittering like everyone else at the fashion house.

Arm in arm, Alice and Aunt Millicent walked over to Barbie and Ken.

"So," said Aunt Millicent, "you must be Ken! I'm Barbie's aunt Millicent and this is Alice. A pleasure to meet you." Aunt Millicent pulled Ken over and hugged him.

"It's nice to meet you, too," said Ken as Alice smiled warmly.

But their moment was cut short as the hot dog restaurant owner cleared his throat loudly. "This is great and all, but unless you've got a huge pile of money for me, I'm still tearing this place down in the morning," the man yelled.

The Flairies gasped. They had all

forgotten about the money! Would they have enough to save the fashion house and the Flairies? Just then, the owner of one of the most famous clothing stores in Paris walked up to Aunt Millicent.

"It was an amazing show, Millicent," said the head of the fashion store. "And to prove it, I'd like to place an order right now. For ten thousand pieces!"

"Ten thousand pieces?!" Alice shouted. "From this line? From *our* line?!"

"Absolutely!" The head of the store nodded. "I can write you a check immediately."

Barbie and Alice were so happy.

"That would be lovely," said Aunt Millicent. "Please make the check out to the giant hot dog." Aunt Millicent pointed to the man dressed in the hot dog costume.

The head of the fashion store thanked her and went to talk to the large hot dog.

"That's it!" Barbie said. "We did it! We saved Millicent's, and we saved the Flairies' power."

"Magic happens when you believe in yourself," Alice said as she looked out onto the smiling crowd. Barbie and Alice waved to the Flairies.

Then the most famous fashion critic in Paris, Lilliana Roxelle, stood up to address the crowd. "Ladies and gentlemen," she said, "I believe this Fashion Fairytale will live happily ever after!" The crowd roared and applauded. "I'd love for you all to come to my Black, White, and Pink Party tonight."

Barbie glowed with excitement. "We'd love to come!"

As everyone left for the party, Jacqueline

and Delphine came over to talk to Barbie, Alice, and Aunt Millicent.

"That was a wonderful show," Jacqueline said to Alice.

"No thanks to you," Alice answered.

"This is true." Jacqueline frowned. "And we—*I*—apologize. Seeing your line, it has a passion I have never known. I wish I hadn't been so awful to you. I would have loved to have worked together." Jacqueline looked at the Flairies. "And maybe have learned something." Jacqueline turned away.

Aunt Millicent went after Jacqueline as she started to leave. "Jacqueline, wait," Aunt Millicent called to her. "We accept your apology. Your designs might be copies, but they are not without talent. Perhaps we can all work together sometime."

Jacqueline bowed her head. "Thank you.

Thank you so much," she said. And she really meant it.

"It's almost time for the Black, White, and Pink Party," Alice reminded everyone. "Are you ready?"

The Flairies joined the group.

Shyne stopped next to Ken. "You must be Barbie's boyfriend. I approve!" she said. She tried to shake his hand, but Ken was too shocked to speak.

"Yes!" Barbie smiled. "Come on, everyone!" The group headed outside where two fancy black, white, and pink limousines waited to take them to the party being held at a castle. Glimmer thought her magic could make the limousines even more fabulous, so she shot Flairy dust over the cars.

Instead of fading into tiny sparkles, the

two cars turned into two gorgeous horse-
drawn carriages!

"Glimmer! That was amazing!" Shyne
hugged her. "Do you realize what you're
doing? Your magic works when you
transform things into something new.
You're a designer!"

"I'm a designer?" Then she smiled and

added, "I'm a designer! Come, your newly designed carriages await!" The group stared at the carriages with wide eyes.

"I knew you could do it!" Barbie exclaimed. "When you believe in yourself, magic really does happen!" She looked over at Alice and Aunt Millicent. "I want to thank all of my friends, new and old, for reminding me of that. Now I'm ready to go back to L.A. and make some magic of my own!"